MONSTER HIGH™

YOU'RE INVITED!

pretty scary parties

An Activity Journal for Ghouls

Written by
**POLLYGEIST
DANESCARY**

LITTLE, BROWN AND COMPANY
NEW YORK BOSTON

IT'S PARTY TIME!

It's time to party, Monster High-style! Your ghoulfriends from Monster High have tricks and treats to help you throw all kinds of amazingly monstrous mashes. Skelebrate howlidays, birthdays, and more with guides to creating your own fangtastic fashion, playing ghostly games, and making spooky snacks.

Turn the page if you're ready to get your pretty scary party on!

THE PARTY OF YOUR SCREAMS

Every ghoul loves a good party! And any excuse to have a party is a good excuse, whether you're celebrating a howliday, turning Sweet 1600, or rewarding yourself for an A in G-ogre-phy.

What is your favorite reason to have a party?
My favorite reason is to meet new friends.

What are your three favorite party games?
1 Molopily
2 Guess Who
3 Head Bandz

What are the beast three songs to listen to at a party?
1 Butiful
2 Scream and Shout
3 Rough Waters

Describe your most fangtastic fantasy party. Where would it be? What decorations would you use? What would you eat and drink? What games would you play? Let your imagination go batty!

My party will be in a big mansion is Florida. The decorations will be ribbons that are blue and the table clothes are white and the bows are purple. And we would eat pizza and chips. Also, play truth or dare, Would you rather and head Bandz.

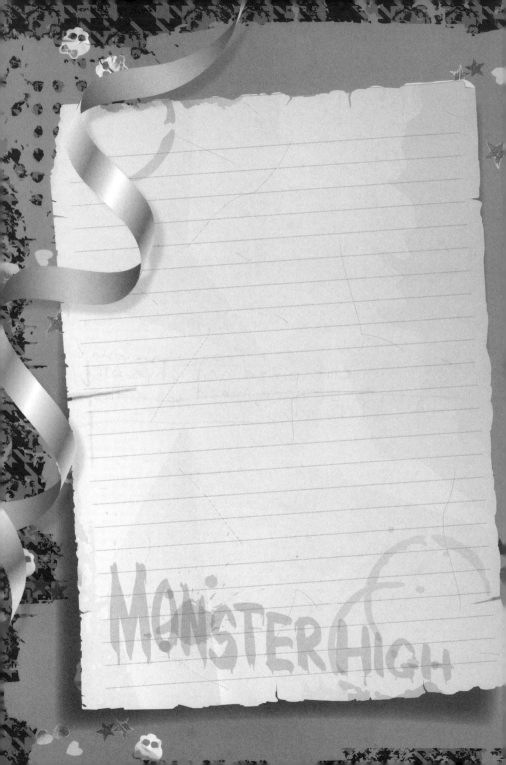

SO THIS CENTURY...

I GOT MAD SKILLS

PRETTY SCARY PARTY PREP

The first step to putting on a killer party of your own is laying the ghostly groundwork. When will your party be? How do you get your digs ready? What spooky skills should a good ghostess have? Read on to find out!

Parties

are so voltage! Getting together with all my ghoulfriends to do exciting new things (everything is exciting and new to me!) really zaps my bolts. When I feel like it's time for a party, the first thing I do is decide what I want to skelebrate!

What are some things you like to skelebrate?
- Birthdays
- Exciting Moments
- Congrjlation Parties

What's your
favorite
howliday?

Chrismas

Sweet 15

What's the best
pretty scary
party you've
attended?

Which of your ghoulfriends do you like to have parties with?

Bella and Anga

Next, I ask my scarents when I can turn my dad's lab—aka the Fab!—into Party Central. To be really persuasive, I tell them why I want to have the party and what I'll do to help with preparations and cleanup.

Write a letter to your scarents telling them why you're so sparked about having a party and how you'll help out.

I ▓▓▓▓▓ could help
you by your clothes and make-up.
 And you throwing a party is hard
because you have to have the looks
the voice and the sound. That means look
pretty, have a good scence and have a
good D.J. and good songs.

 P.S.
 Have "BOYS". Also, a slow

dance.

SCARENTAL UNITS: ENGAGE

Put your scarents to work! Ask your scarents to help brainstorm decorations, plan a menu, make snacks, and organize party activities and games. Maybe you'll even learn something new about them! Try interviewing your scarents to see how they can help out.

INTERVIEW

What's the beast party you've ever thrown or attended? What made it spooktacular?

I thrown a sweet 16. It was spooktacular, because it haved boys and pretty dresses.

What are your secret party skills?

Have the look the voivce and the sound.

What are your favorite party activities?

~~scribbled out~~ truth or dare
and would you rather.

Now that you've interviewed them, you and your scarents can
list some ideas for how they can participate:

PRETTY SCARY PARTY PREP: INFRIGHTATIONS

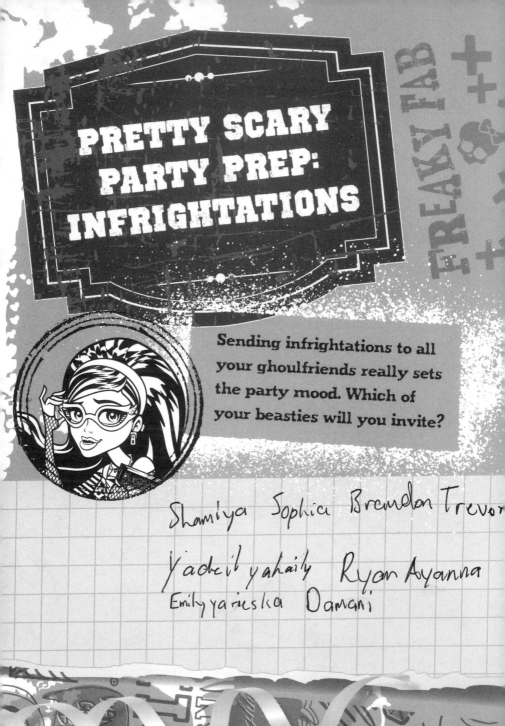

Sending infrightations to all your ghoulfriends really sets the party mood. Which of your beasties will you invite?

Shamiya   Sophia   Brendan   Trevor

Yadeil yahaily   Ryan Ayanna

Emily yarieska   Damani

INFRIGHTATIONS

Maul-bought or homemade?

Do you want to send maul-bought infrightations, fresh from the package and perfectly printed? Or would you prefer to make infrights of your own, each one a mini monsterpiece? Time to make a list of pros and cons!

Maul-bought

Pros:

* super professional
* can add ghoulgeous touches with the help of a little glue

I would touch with glue.

Cons:

* a bit less personal
* may not exactly match party theme

A bit less personal

HOMEMADE (ON THE COMPUTER OR BY HAND!)

Pros:

* super boo-nique
* can be tailored to your theme

Can be tailored to your theme

Cons:

* time-consuming
* might need to try different designs

time-consuming

INFRIGHTATION BASICS

WHEN SHOULD YOU SEND YOUR INFRIGHTATIONS?

The more formal the event, the earlier you should send out infrightations. Between Fearleading practice, Dragonomics homework, and family time, your ghoulfriends are *très* busy, and you will need to give them enough time to plan. Send infrights anytime—from the day of the party (because you simply must have a soiree this minute!) to a month in advance. Try to send them at least two weeks before the party if possible.

Do you want to use e-mail or scale mail? It's up to you! It really depends on the type of party you're throwing and how much time you have. Add some pros and cons to these lists!

E-MAIL

Pros:
★ quick and easy
★ oh soooo *moderne*

Oh soooo moderne
_____
_____

Cons:
★ not as elegant
★ can't show off
   penmanship skills
_____
_____
_____

SCALE MAIL

Pros:
★ old-ghoul-style
★ adds a personal touch

adds a personal
touch
_____

Cons:
★ takes longer to send
★ more work to make
_____
_____

WHAT INFORMATION DO YOU NEED TO INCLUDE?

What are you celebrating?
Birthday

Day, date, and time? 8/30   6:30
August 30

Location?   8/30/14
Keating Home

RSVP date? -
_____

Appropriate attire (if applicable)?
_____

RSVP stands for répondez, s'il vous plaît, which is French for "please reply." According to paragraph 11.27 of the Gargoyle Code of Ethics, infrightees need to accept or decline an infrightation by the RSVP date.

KEEPING UP YOUR DIGS

A good ghostess makes her ghoulfriends feel welcome by tidying up her digs. Make sure to check off everything on your cleaning list. And, of course, you should play some music and turn your cleaning session into a howling dance party!

SCREAM CLEANING

After everything is spick-and-span, you can set up your party supplies, turning your digs into a monsterific party plaza!

- ☑ Sweep up deadly dust bunnies.
- ☑ Clean your dragon's litter box.
- ☑ Pick up things around the house.
- ☑ Clean your room. (At least give anything messy to the monster in your closet.)
- ☑ Put away the dishes in the kitchen.
- ☑ Don't forget yourself—take a beastly bath!
- ☑ Fix you bed
- ☑ Then watch tv

FANG TASTIC

GETTING IT PARTY READY

☑ Set up a table with snacks and nibbles. If you're making any tasty treats in advance, be sure they're ready on time.

☑ Arrange your ghoulish games and activities area. Check to make sure all the supplies you might need are set out.

☑ Prep your pretty scary playlist.

☑ Will there be a Dance of the Delightfully Dead or other wild and crazy activities? Clear a space so you won't break anything.

☑ Put out your frightfully fabulous decorations! (This is the beast part!)

☐ _____

☐ _____

☐ _____

☐ _____

HOWL ABOUT IT?

FREAKY FAB PARTY SNACKS

At a party, you get to eat fun snacks that you don't have every day. Here are some party snack ideas. Add your own faves to the list!

★ pigs in a shroud
★ monsterella sticks
★ heart-i-choke dip
★ peanut butter and skelery sticks
★ chips and salsa
★ bat wings with buffalo sauce

monsterella sticks
_____
_____

There may be foods that some of your ghoulfriends can't eat. (Draculaura's a vegetarian, so no pigs in a shroud for her!) Ask your guests if there are any foods they can't eat so you can have something for everyone. You can also find out their favorites! Record your notes here for future reference!

Ghoulfriend: Shamiya   Can't eat: Kiwi   Loves to eat: Monsterella sti

Ghoulfriend: Kaila   Can't eat: Shell fish   Loves to eat: Pizza

Ghoulfriend: Emily   Can't eat: _____   Loves to eat: _____

Ghoulfriend: Yadeil   Can't eat: _____   Loves to eat: _____

Ghoulfriend: Brandon   Can't eat: _____   Loves to eat: _____

Ghoulfriend: Trevon   Can't eat: _____   Loves to eat: _____

GHOSTERY LIST

When you're ready to go shopping for ingredients, remember to take this list with you!

DEFRIGHTFUL DECORATIONS

Choosing party decorations is so exciting! You can make everything look so *bonita* if you use your imagination! You can use crepe paper, streamers, balloons, construction paper, papier-mâché—whatever you wish.

Jot down some freaky fab decoration ideas!

streamers   boun Pictures
sparkles   disco ball

GHOSTESS ETIQUETTE

The most important thing to remember is that you want your ghoulfriends to have a wonderful time and feel comfortable *chez vous*. To make everyone feel *magnifique*, offer ghouls beverages as they arrive, introduce ghouls who haven't met each other, and have a designated place for ghouls to leave their coats, bags, and iCoffins.

To welcome ghouls monster-party-style, make up a rock-solid greeting to say to them as they arrive. Write some greeting ideas below!

Welcome to the
scariest party ever.
And if you got invited
you are to ghoul for school

Remember to make you guests feel spooktacula during the party, and your fete will be sure to be a smash hit!

LET'S GET THIS PRETTY SCARY PARTY STARTED!

It's time to pick your freaktacular theme and get the party going with activities, games, and more. Be creative, get crazy, and party like a Scarisian! On the next page are some great ideas for skelebrating birthdays!

Zombies

BIRTHDAYS

Your birthday is your very own howliday, so you should skelebrate in spookerific-style. Whether it's with chic gauze bandages, fab freshwater party games, or monster makeovers, this will be a party to remember!

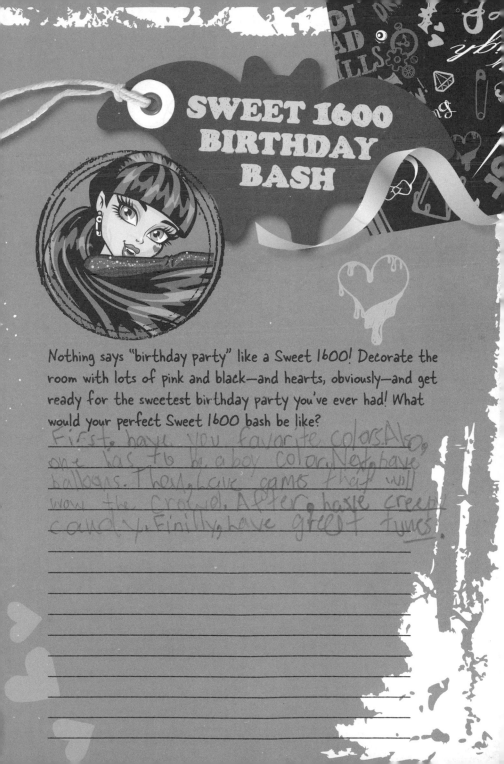

SWEET 1600 BIRTHDAY BASH

Nothing says "birthday party" like a Sweet 1600! Decorate the room with lots of pink and black—and hearts, obviously—and get ready for the sweetest birthday party you've ever had! What would your perfect Sweet 1600 bash be like?

First, have you favorite colors. Also, one has to be a boy color. Next, have balloans. Then, have games that will wow the crowd. After, have creepy candy. Finilly, have great tunes!

PRETTY SCARY PRESENTS

Birthday presents are the beast! We all love getting something new and exciting. Here are a few tips for opening them.

Start with the present closest to you. Don't pick through the pile; you'll get to open them all, don't worry! After you open each present, thank the ghoulfriend who gave it to you. Any present you get is a thoughtful gesture; be appreciative of your fangtastic friends. Once the party's over, write thank-you notes to your ghoulfriends for the gifts...just like everyone did 1,600 years ago.

Draft a Sweet 1600-worthy thank-you note here!

Dear Jada,
thank you for the jean and the Hello kitty shirt

love, Kaila

Dear _____,
_____
_____
_____
_____
_____
_____

Dear Grandma and Grandpa,
thank you for the present

Love, Kaila

Dear _____,
_____
_____
_____
_____
_____

BIRTHDAY SPOOKTACULAR

Name some pharaohific things that make you feel like a birthday queen!

A spotlight. A chair. Some lights. Ballet ,oter Crown, Queen and King. Date.

A PARTY

A party that will make you say
"Oh my ra" has got to have a
killer playlist. Try these songs,
and add some of your own.
"Call Me Mummy"
"Some Frights"
"What Makes You Bootiful"

"22"
"When I was
your man"
"Roalal"

"Wrecking
Ball"

DRESS LIKE A QUEEN!

To be truly pharaohnic, you need to dress like a pharaoh, which means it's time to be mummified. Divide into two teams for this preservation competition! (You'll need several rolls of toilet paper.)

Instructions:

1. Each team picks one ghoul to be the pharaoh. (If you play multiple rounds, you can take turns being the pharaoh.)
2. The pharaoh stands in the middle of her team.
3. On the count of three, each team has to mummify the pharaoh by wrapping her completely—except her face—in toilet paper!
4. The team that turns their pharaoh into a mummy first wins!
5. Whip out your iCoffins. You're going to want to preserve these images forever!

Draw your own versions of the mummy pictures you took here. You can try to re-create the pictures exactly, or you can let your imagination go wild!

CREEPOVER BIRTHDAY PARTY

What could be better than an all-night birthday party? Stock up on some voltage snacks and monster makeover supplies, learn some secrets about your ghoulfriends, and break out the sparky decorations, complete with black and white crepe paper. This birthday creepover will be one to scream about!

What are your favorite things to do at a creepover party?

Board Games, Baking, Beauty. Movies¾ Popcorn; Pillow Fights

Who would you invite to spend a bolt-popping night at your Fab?

Totally VOLTAGE

SPARKYLICIOUS

What's the sparkiest thing you've every done at a creepover party?

CUPCAKEOVER

You'll definitely need some sustenance to keep your batteries charged all night long. So prep some unfrosted cupcakes before your ghoulfriends come over, then give the cupcakes alternative makeovers together. You'll need the unfrosted cupcakes; white frosting; food coloring; licorice sticks, chocolate chips, cinnamon candies and other candies for decorations; one bowl and spoon per ghoul; and a frosting piper (a bag with a metal or plastic tip).

Use your toppings to create ghoulammed-up cupcakes. Make different frosting colors by mixing small amounts of the white frosting with a drop or two of food coloring. Give your cupcakes hair, eyes (with eye shadow!), ears (with earrings!), noses, rouged cheeks, and lipsticked lips.

Draw some sweet designs for your ghoulamorous cupcakes here!

MONSTER MAKEOVERS

SKIN SCARE

You've got to take care of your skin, mate, if you want to keep it smooth and healthy after lots of outdoor hang time. Give your face a vibrant glow with a relaxing face mask. Put on some fintastic music and get out the cucumbers!

You'll need:

★ daily cleanser
★ 1 regular-size tube of mud mask (should be enough for four ghouls)
★ 1 cucumber, sliced

GHOUL RULE!!

Instructions:

1. Make sure your hair is off your face. Ghouls with long hair should pull it up into a bun to keep it out of the way. Ghouls with shorter hair can clip it back or use a headband.
2. To make sure the mud mask won't irritate anyone's skin, each ghoul should put some on her wrist and leave it there for at least 15 minutes, then wash it off. If any ghoul's skin shows signs of irritation, she should skip the mud mask. (But she can still use the cucumbers!)
3. Wash your face with the cleanser.
4. Apply the mud mask to your face (steer clear of the eyes!) and set a timer for 20 minutes. Everyone's scales will be smooth and ghoulgeous soon!
5. Lie down and place a slice of cucumber on each eye. This is a great time for a Gossip Ghoul session.
6. Remember to take lots of pictures of your ghostly mud mask faces! When the timer goes off, throw away the cucumbers (definitely don't eat them!) and wash your face.

What a ghoulgeous glow!

What's a freaky fab look you've been dying to try?

Get your
ghoulfriends
to help you
try it out!

MAUL OF AMERICA

Time for a freaky fab wardrobe update? It's time to raid your ghoulfriends' closets, because one ghoul's "done with this" is another ghoul's "can't wait to wear it!"

So have every ghoul bring the clothes she doesn't want to wear anymore, pull out the full-length mirrors, and set up some snacks. It's a good idea to have a wish list prepared before you go "shopping." What claw-some clothes would you really like to score?

_____
_____
_____
_____

What are some of your dream outfits? Include a mix of clothes you already own and clothes you wish you had!

_____
_____
_____
_____

MAUL PREP

When your ghoulfriends arrive, start by skimming through magazines like *Sevenscream*, *Teen Ghoul*, and even *American Fearleader* and tearing out pages with claw-some outfits—the better to inspire you with!

HOWLABOUT IT?

SHOP UNTIL YOU DROP DEAD

Then toss all your unwanted clothes in a pile. Sort the clothes by type (pants, shirts, skirts). Now pick out some new threads from the heap. You may have to haggle if you and another ghoul are eyeing the same piece.

BF

GETTING TO KNOW BOO!

You may think you know everything about your ghoulfriends, but there are probably a few facts that you've never even thought to ask about. (Or maybe you've forgotten about them. Remembering every little thing is like trying to hold on to a goldfish!) Here are some questions to get you started.

What's your favorite song to sing in the shower?
What is your freaky flaw?
What movie do you know all the words to?
What's your favorite toothpaste flavor?

Now add some questions of your own!
_____
_____
_____
_____
_____

SWIMMING WITH THE FISHIES BIRTHDAY

Hey, mate, for a sunny summer birthday bash, break out the screech towels, swimsuits, and a few screech balls, and you're ready for a fintastic time in the pool! Add some twinkly lights to the pool fence for a freshwater grotto effect, and be prepared with ice scream and hamburgers. Flapping your fins really works up an appetite!

Safety tip:
Ask an adult to stay nearby while you and your mates are in or around the pool!

Some of my favorite summer tunes are "Summer of Fishy-Nine," "Summer Frights," and "Itsy Bitsy Teenie Weenie Yellow Polkascare Bikini." What are yours? Make a fishy party playlist!

Hey, Gills!

What fintastic water games can you play to keep cool, in the pool and out?

SO THIS CENTURY...

I GOT MAD SKILLS

SAFE SKIN IN THE SUN

SKIN-SCARE TIPS:

Playing games in the pool is tons of fun, but it can be rough on your scales. You need to put skin scare first.

★ Apply a waterproof sunscream.

★ Stay hydrated! Drink lots of liquids, especially water. (But, uh, not pool water.)

★ Don't stay in direct sunlight too long. Take a break and spend some time lounging under an umbrella or a covered area and chatting with your ghoulfriends.

★ Pop on a hat if you've been out for a while. The skin on your face is extrasensitive!

★ Awfully important: Even when it's cloudy out, the water in your pool reflects sunlight, and you can burn more easily than when no water is nearby. So reapply sunscream every hour no matter what!

POLTERNALITY QUIZ

While you're resting in the shade, take this quiz with your friends before you jump back in the pool. Are you most like a vampire, a dragon, or a sea monster? Let's find out!

1. Before you go anywhere, what do you check in the mirror?
   a. your outfit, to make sure it looks as creative as you feel
   b. your skin, to confirm that you're sufficiently moisturized
   c. nothing—no mirror can truly reflect your beauty
2. What is your favorite activity?
   a. painting, sewing, writing—you love to express yourself
   b. swimming, playing soccer, playing Casketball—athletics make you feel great
   c. shopping, experimenting with makeup, talking to your ghoulfriends—you love to pamper yourself and bond with your pals
3. What is your dream scarecation?
   a. going to Scaris to see all the ghoulgeous artwork
   b. frolicking in the waves with your ghoulfriends on a Hexican screech. Bright blue waters as far as the eye can see!
   c. exploring Screamattle—quaint shopping, not too much sun, and lots of lattes

4. What do you look for in a beast friend?
    a. someone who is scary supportive
    b. someone who loves to be active
    c. someone who loves to talk on the phone all night
5. What is your favorite subject in school (if you had to choose one!)?
    a. Ghoulish Literature
    b. Physical Deaducation
    c. Biteology

If you chose mostly *As*, you're most like a Dragon! You're creative and love getting inspired by objects of beauty. Just be sure to make enough time for your ghoulfriends!

If you chose mostly *Bs*, you're most like a Sea Monster! You love to splish, splash, and have a good time. Keep having fintastic fun, but add in some relaxing activities to strike a healthy balance.

If you chose mostly *Cs*, you're most like a Vampire! You don't love the sun, but you do love spending time with your ghoulfriends and taking care of yourself. You may need to add a little room into your schedule for studying—but don't stop having a great time with your beasties!

HEART-Y TEA BIRTHDAY PARTY

Tea and crumpets do a birthday ghoul good! Victerrorian Fangland was sooooo romantic. When Queen Victerroria reigned in Fangland, they had parties just like in some of my favorite books (*Fright and Prejudice, Great Hexpectations*), with live musicians, dancing, and reciting of poetry by William Spooksfear, Ben Jekyllson, and Sir Walterror Scott. Today, any Victerrorian birthday shindig worth its fangs will come complete with teensy sandwiches, scarylicious scones, and pots and pots of tea.

Get in the aristobatic spirit by creating fancy Fanglish names for you and your ghoulfriends! Fanglish Aristobats:

Lady Draculaura the Fourth _____

Duchess Cleo of Egyptshire _____

Countess Clawdeen Wolf _____

The Honorable Fearess Frankie Stein _____

William Spooksfear is beast known for writing plays (hello, *Romeo and Ghouliet*), but he also wrote sonnets, which are a type of poem. Write some poems of your own as a group, using the opening lines below to get started.

Sit in a circle. Ghoul A (the birthday ghoul!) reads the opening line, then makes up a line of her own that rhymes with it. The ghoul to her left then makes up a rhyming line, and so on around the circle. Try not to repeat words, but don't worry if you do. And the poem can make sense, but it doesn't have to! Once everyone has added a line, start over with a new opening line (and a new Ghoul A).

LOL

Here's a hexample:

★ Opening line: We all go to Monster High.
★ Ghoul A: We tell the truth; we never lie.
★ Ghoul B: We like to snack on apple pie.
★ Ghoul C: We like to laugh but not to cry.

Start off with one of these opening lines:

★ I think I saw a little bat.
★ Lagoona loves the big blue sea.
★ The Maul will have the perfect store.
★ Tie your fur up in a bow.
★ Monsters rock. I think that's clear.
★ We've got spirit; yes, we do.

Now write your own opening lines here. Make sure to end with a word that rhymes with a lot of other words.

SO THIS CENTURY...

HEART-Y TEA

A good tea party is about more than just bites to eat! You should set the mood with some nice classical music. (The soundtracks to Jane Austen movies are a good choice.) And visit some thrift stores, craft stores, and costume stores to select some fangtastic accessories. Set the items out on a table so you and your ghoulfriends can get dressed up before you sit down to tea. You can also get some perfectly mismatched teacups and saucers at the thrift store.

Accessory ideas:
* freaky feather boas
* chic hats
* old-ghoul gloves
* ghoulamorous jewelry
* lace handkerchiefs

Tea is a formal occasion, so be on your beast behavior! Quick tips:

★ Milk and sugar should be on the table for each ghoul to add if she wants.

★ The teapot's spout should point toward the ghostess.

★ Don't clink your spoon against your teacup as you stir.

★ Leave your saucer on the table when you lift your teacup.

★ You may have heard otherwise, but here's the truth: To be truly skelegant, keep your pinkie in, not out!

The nibbles you serve at tea are monstrously important—and they're the perfect backdrop for bonding with your ghoulfriends. Every tea party should have bite-size sandwiches, scones, and desserts. Plan your heart-y teatime menu here!

WANNA GRAB A BITE?

SCARY Liciou>

To give your ghoulfriends the aristobatic treatment, you'll need to give them some scarylicious options for their tea drinking. Take this quiz with your ghoulfriends to find out what flavor your taste buds will like beast!

1. What is your dream pet?
   a. fiery dragon
   b. nocturnal owl
   c. wee woolly mammoth
   d. cuddly bat

2. What is your favorite perfume scent?
   a. something spicy and adventurous
   b. a flowery, romantic blend
   c. something that smells cozy and comforting
   d. sweet and soothing

3. If you could have any career, what would it be?
   a. extreme athlete
   b. wildlife biteologist
   c. writer of ghoulish literature
   d. pretty scary party planner

4. What do you do after school?
   a. I always have an extracurricular, whether it's the Fearbook, Casketball, Fearleading, or something else.
   b. I like to ride my bike around the neighborhood or maybe stop by Gloom Beach.
   c. After I finish my Clawculus homework, I like to curl up with a good book or watch TV.
   d. I always make time to talk to my ghoulfriends on my iCoffin.

5. What is your favorite snack?
   a. nuts (like pistachighosts, peanuts, and cash-ews)
   b. fruit (like scareberries, oranges, and abominapples)
   c. anything chocolaty
   d. cheese crackers

★ If you chose mostly As, you should try Indian chai! You're adventurous and seek out the exciting things in unlife. Add plenty of milk and sugar to bring out the warm, spicy flavor of your tea.

★ If you chose mostly Bs, you should try chamomile tea! You love to take in the ghoulgeous nature all around you. Add a little sugar to your tea, but no milk—that would dilute the sweet, flowery taste.

★ If you chose mostly Cs, you should try peppermint tea! You're a big fan of staying in on rainy days and getting lots of introspectration. Add some milk and sugar to make your tea taste like a peppermint candy.

★ If you chose mostly Ds, you should try black vanilla tea! You're sweet, but not too sweet, and you love your ghoulfriends, but also enjoy spending time on your own. Add only a little bit of sugar to your tea so you don't cover the warm vanilla flavor, and add some milk if you want it to be a little creamy.

FREAKY FLASHBACK TO THE '80S BIRTHDAY PARTY

Blue eye shadow, multiple pairs of socks, and neon legging will take you and your ghoulfriends back in time to the '80s Better yet, ask everyone to dress like Monsterdonna: black and white lace, scary-cool gloves, and lots of necklaces! Hit eBay and thrift stores for '80s movie posters, blast some '80s tunes, and use neon colors everyscare. Neon pink and neon green are pretty vinelicious, if you ask me.

For true authenticity, your '80s party should be an iCoffin-free zone. Try to make it for a whole night without texting anyone!

Who knows all about the '80s? Your scarents, of course! Pump them for information about the decadent decade. You can also get the spooky-skinny from aunts, uncles, grandscarents—anyone who can remember life before the Internet. Pick some interview subjects, and ask them the questions below.

What '80s fashion did you love, and what did you loathe?

What were your favorite '80s movies and TV shows?

What about commercials? Do you remember any funny ones?

What was your favorite and least favorite '80s music? Teach me your dance moves!

What board games and book crazes do you
remember?

What were your favorite snacks?

PIN THE MULLET

ON THE MONSTER

No '80s party is complete without someone sporting a mullet. You are too spooktacular for that particular style, but you can subject a cutout to it! (My own hair is much more plant-punk than a mullet, for the record.) You'll need a drawing or photo of someone with short hair in profile. You can find a photo, or you can draw someone yourself on a piece of poster board.

You and your ghoulfriends need to make some mullets! If your monster is blond, use blond yarn; if brunette, use brown yarn.

You'll need:

★ 4-inch strips of paper

★ 1 skein of yarn

★ blindfold

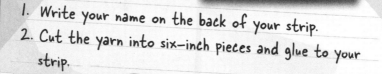

1. Write your name on the back of your strip.
2. Cut the yarn into six-inch pieces and glue to your strip.

3. Allow to dry, then place small pieces of tape on the back of your strip. (You're really going to tape your mullet, not pin it.)

4. Blindfold the first contestant. Turn her around in several circles; when you stop turning her, leave her facing the monster.

5. The contestant will stick her mullet to the poster where she thinks it should go. No touching the wall to try to figure it out!
6. The ghoul with the closest mullet wins!

FRIGHTEOUS MOVIE MADNESS

Pick out an '80s movie to watch to really bring you back in time! Before the movie starts, check out some of the commercials your scarents told you about when you interviewed them!

Movies to Watch

- ★ The Breakfast Club
- ★ The Goonies
- ★ Labyrinth
- ★ The Princess Bride
- ★ Sixteen Candles

BIRTHDAY PARTY REVIEW

It's time for a post-party play-by-play! Which birthday party idea sounds like a total scream to you? Why? Write howl about it here.

FANG
TASTIC

What totally voltage presents did you receive for your last birthday? Which ones meant the most?

GHOSTS OF BIRTHDAYS PAST

Did you have one birthday in particular when you were a small ghoul that was your favorite? Was it when you turned 15 days old, or 1600 years old? Write everything you can remember about it and why it's so special to you here.

MONSTER HIGH

GHOSTS OF BIRTHDAYS PAST

GHOSTS OF BIRTHDAYS PAST

Be yourself
BE UNIQUE

GHOSTS OF
BIRTHDAYS PAST

MONSTER HIGH

GHOULS
RULE!!

HOWLIDAY PARTIES

Skelebrate national—and international—howlidays in style! We've got monster tips for all kinds of skelebrations, from Scarisian to Hexican, patriotic to romantic, and spooky to sparky. There's no howliday party like a Monster High howliday party!

GH

Freaky FAB in EV

FRIDAY THE 13TH PARTY

Skelebrate every Friday the 13th with your ghoulfriends! Decorate by setting out thirteen of each item you choose (they can be anything—candles, abominapples, buttons), and invite twelve ghoulfriends over (plus you is thirteen!) to skelebrate all things thirteen.

As every monster knows, Friday the 13th is all about being lucky. When are times that you've felt lucky?

13 QUESTIONS

A Monster High guessing game that will have you dying of curiosity.

The answer ghoul picks something from Monster High (a character, location, or object—be creative!) and doesn't tell anyone what it is. The group gets thirteen questions total to guess the item. Remember to start out with "Monster, vegetable, or mineral?" to narrow things down. (Another good question might be "Is it bigger than an iCoffin?") After you've guessed (or not guessed!) the answer, it's someone else's turn to be the answer ghoul.

BFF

13 DANCES

Dance the lucky 13th away!
Put on your favorite lucky
music for a mini dance party.
Get in a big circle and take
turns dancing in the middle.
The ghouls in the circle will copy
whatever dance moves the ghoul in the middle is
doing. Once all thirteen ghouls have led a dance,
see if you can remember all thirteen dance
moves—in order! Bonus points for anyone who can
do the Monster High theme song dance!

13

SCAVENGER 13

Since thirteen is such a lucky number, it's always good to gather items in sets of thirteen. This scavenger hunt can be each ghoul for herself, or you can play in teams of two or more. Add your own ideas for items to hunt to the amped-up list below. The first ghoul (or team) to take pictures of thirteen of the items on the list is the winner!

★ bolts (Frankie might need an extra.)

★ Mad Science book

★ potted plant

★ moisturizer (Lagoona can always use some extra!)

★ a copy of *Teen Scream*

★ musical instrument (so Operetta can play a tune)

★ monarch butterfly (one of Skelita's pets!)

★ Clawdeen-worthy shoes

★ sunglasses (in case Deuce misplaces his)

★ glasses (Can you find a style like Ghoulia's?)

★ fur elastic

science

Scary Cet

★

★

★

★

VALENTINE'S DAY SPOOKTACULAR PARTY

What's pink, black, white, and scary-cute all over? A Valentine's Day Spooktacular, created especially for me by Valentine himself! Serve up some pink screamonade and pink sugar cookies, plus a tray of raspberries, scareberries, and grapefruit. (You can drizzle the grapefruit with a little honey if it's too tart for you.) Did I mention that everything should be pink?

Now, Valentine's Day is a good time to think about boys, naturally. Who are your secret special valentines this year?

_____

_____

_____

_____

_____

LOVE

Write some
spooky sweet
valentines of
your own!

XOXO

XoXo

OMG

MONSTER MASH

On Valentine's Day, you're simply dying to know what your future holds. A round of Monster MASH will give you a little glimpse!

MASH (Monster Mansion, Amoaning Apartment, Spooky Shack, or Haunted House) will reveal fun fortunes, like where you'll live, who you'll marry, how many kids you'll have, what your profession will be, and what color and kind of car you'll drive. Talk about a freaky sneak peek!

One ghoul at a time will play the game, but everyone will get a turn. On a sheet of paper, copy down the categories listed on the chart below. With your ghoulfriends' help, write down four things for each category: four people you might marry, four cars you might drive, four car colors, four places you might live, and four jobs you might have. For "Number of Kids," write 1, 2, 3, and 4. Now close your eyes and draw a spiral. When your ghoulfriends shout, "Stop!" you can count the lines in the spiral from the top to the bottom. This is your MASH number. Starting with the M (for Monster Mansion), count clockwise (to the right) through your lists. Cross out the item that you land on each time you count to your MASH number. When only one item is left in a category, circle it. Now you know your Monster MASH!

M. A. S. H.

MARRIED TO

MONSTER CARS

car colors

PLACES TO LIVE

SCAREERS

NUMBER OF KIDS

M.A.S.H.

MARRIED TO   MONSTER CARS   car colors

PLACES TO LIVE   SCAREERS   NUMBER OF KIDS

M.A.S.H.

MARRIED TO   MONSTER CARS   car colors

PLACES TO LIVE   SCAREERS   NUMBER OF KIDS

M.A.S.H.

MARRIED TO	MONSTER CARS	car colors

PLACES TO LIVE	SCAREERS	NUMBER OF KIDS

M.A.S.H.

MARRIED TO	MONSTER CARS	car colors

PLACES TO LIVE	SCAREERS	NUMBER OF KIDS

HEARTS ON (JINA)FIRE

Make some claw-some hearts to give to your friends and family members.

MONSTER HIGH

You'll need:

★ crayons (new or used)
★ silicone heart candy molds
★ plastic craft bags
★ paper (for making gift tags)
★ craft scissors (with
   patterned blades)

★ regular scissors
★ hole punch
★ curling craft ribbon
   in wild shades and
   patterns

Heart Instructions:

1. With an adult's help, preheat your oven to 275°F.
2. Set one box of crayons aside to use for gift tags.
3. Gather all the ghouls together to peel the paper off
   the rest of the crayons.
4. Break each crayon into three or four pieces.
5. Place several crayon pieces (about a crayon's worth) into
   each mold.
6. You can make solid-colored hearts or mix up the colors!
   But if you use too many colors in one mold, they'll blend
   together, so stick to two or three colors at the most.
7. With an adult's help, bake the hearts for 10 to
   12 minutes.
8. Allow to cool and set; once they're cool, pop them out
   of the molds!

Who will you give
valentines to
this year?

Happy Cute...

GREEN SCENE: EARTH DAY PARTY

Help keep Venus's vined friends all over the world in tip-top shape with this pollen-tastic party. Drape the room in green, green, and more green—preferably recycled—and have a freaky fab time.

Check out these oxygenerific reasons for skelebrating Earth, and add some reasons of your own!

* The planet provides us with ghoulgeous natural scenery to look at and enjoy.
* Delicious fresh food and clean water come from the world around us.
* Some natural resources, like trees, are renewable; planting enough trees helps regulate the carbon monsteroxide in the atmosphere.
* Other natural resources, like petroleum, aren't renewable; limiting our use of them makes them last longer.
* Using recycled paper products can help make sure that animals like Chewy and Sir Hoots A Lot—and their wild-animal cousins—have places to live.
* Conserving energy can help stop the polar ice caps from melting so the polar bears and other cold-weather animals won't become extinct.

KEEP IT GREEN

HOWL
ABOUT
IT?

Getting down with
nature is the beast!
Draw your own
vinetastic garden
hideaway here.

Scary Cute

FREAKY CHIC FLOWERS

Plant your own temporary garden with another snack: flowers! Because sometimes it's okay to play with your food...and create a garden of ideas for your next veggie snack attack.

You'll need cucumber slices, fresh spinach leaves, cherry tomatoes, baby carrots, celery sticks, radish slices, and ranch dressing. And don't forget to find a big plate to use as your "canvas."

Go crazy! Use the veggies to design gardenscapes, boo-quets, flowers with Monster High ghouls' faces—whatever comes to mind. You can work together on a big flower mural, or you can each make your own mini monsterpiece. Take a picture of your creations, then eat the veggies with the ranch dressing as a yummy dip.

MONSTER HIGH

HIDE-AND-SCREECH

Conserve some energy with a game of hide-and-screech—in the dark! The more energy you save, the better off plants and animals are.

Instructions:

1. Turn off every light in the house and close all the curtains.

2. Pick a ghoul to be the screecher. She'll start the game at the haunted home base.

3. While the screecher counts to ten, all the other ghouls hide.

4. When the screecher says, "Ready or not, here I creep!" make sure you're hidden. The screecher's job is to find all the hidden ghouls. The ghouls can try to reach haunted home base without getting caught, or they can count on the screecher not finding them.

5. The round is over when the last ghoul is found or caught.

6. The first ghoul to be caught by the screecher becomes the screecher for the next round.

HEXICAN FIESTA

Break out the red, white, and green for a Hexican fiesta! Serve up some casketdillas and brush up on your *español*! Practice these words and phrases with your ghoulfriends!

Hello!	¡Hola!
How are you?	¿Cómo estás?
I'm fine, thanks. And you?	Bien gracias. ¿Y tú?
What's your name?	¿Cómo te llamas?
My name is...	Me llamo...
Good morning	¡Buenos días!
Good afternoon	¡Buenas tardes!
Good night	¡Buenas noches!
Good-bye	¡Adiós!
Cheers	¡Salud!
Have a nice day!	¡Que pase un buen día!
I don't understand.	No entiendo. / No comprendo.
A little	Un poco
How much is this?	¿Cuánto cuesta?

HEXICAN HAT DANCE

Do some *bonita* dancing with your very own Hexican hat dance to skelebrate Hexican scaritage. Before your party, cue up some Hexican hat dance videos to give you some choreography ideas.

Hat Dance Tips:

★ Break up into pairs and choreograph duets.

★ Include a slow opening, then leap into quicker action.

★ Choreograph in counts of four.

★ Make sure to incorporate some twirls.

★ Don't forget the footwork! Lots of heel-toe action goes into a good hat dance.

PARTY PREP: CASKETDILLAS

Cheesy casketdillas will fill a whole crowd of skeletons up!
These have to be served hot, so you'll need an adult's help.
You can make them before the party, then just heat them
up right before eating; or you can have everything prepared
and cook them during the party.

You'll need (for two ghouls):
- ★ butter or cooking spray
- ★ 2 large flour tortillas
- ★ 1 cup grated cheddar cheese
- ★ salsa
- ★ sour cream
- ★ 8 ounces chopped, cooked chicken (optional)

Instructions:
1. In a frying pan large enough for a tortilla to lay flat, spray cooking spray or heat butter so the entire bottom of the pan is greased.
2. Place one tortilla in the pan on low to medium heat, and allow to brown slightly. Set this tortilla aside.
3. Place the second tortilla in the pan. Immediately sprinkle the grated cheese over the tortilla. If you're using chicken, scatter the chicken on top of the cheese.
4. Place the first tortilla on top of the cheese, browned side up.
5. Press the tortillas together with a spatula.
6. Fry until the cheese is melted, then remove from the pan. Cut into wedges like a pizza.
7. Serve salsa and sour cream on the side.

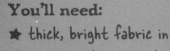

Using bright fabrics and ghostly skills, sew your very own handbag—complete with some skelegant embroidery. Be unique!

You'll need:

* thick, bright fabric in various patterns and colors (scraps or new)
* colorful yarn
* bright ribbon
* yarn needles
* scissors
* measuring tape
* pins
* white embroidery thread
* embroidery needle

1. Pick some fabric you like and lay it out so you have two sides that are 8" x 6". Each side can be made up of a single piece of fabric or multiple pieces.
2. If your sides have multiple pieces, you'll use yarn and a yarn needle to stitch the pieces together.

3. To stitch the pieces, first tie a knot in the end of the yarn. Holding the two pieces you're sewing together with their edges overlapping, push the needle up from the wrong side of the fabric to the right side, with the needle going through both pieces of fabric. Then bring the yarn down one-eighth of an inch away, through both pieces of fabric. Keep doing this until the pieces are stitched together.

4. When both pieces are assembled, place the two sides together, right sides facing each other. Pin the sides so the edges are lined up.

5. Using the yarn and yarn needle again, stitch the eight-inch sides together; then stitch just one of the six-inch sides together. Remove the pins.

6. Cut a piece of ribbon to the desired length, and stitch it to both sides of the opening for a handle.

7. Turn the bag right side out.

8. Using the embroidery needle and the white embroidery thread, stitch a simple heart shape in the center of one side of the bag. To do this, use medium-size stitches to outline a heart. Then use stitches of varying lengths to create a scribbling effect inside the heart.

Design your own custom Hexican handbag here. If you're feeling *muy* brave, break out the craft supplies and make your bag come to unlife. It's a limited edition!

MONSTER HIGH

FOURTH OF GHOULY PARTY

Hang the banner for the most patriotic day of the year. On the Fourth of Ghouly, Amerighosts remember the signing of the Declaration of In-dead-pendence, which separated the USA from Fangland. Red, white, and blue will put you in the mood, and traditional treats like pigs in a shroud and watermelon will keep you fueled for a whole day of skelebrations. Scares and stripes forever!

Fourth of Ghouly skelebrations can mean watching frighterworks, swimming in the pool, having a barbecue, and more. What are some of your favorite Ghouly Fourth memories? Do they give you any ideas for things you could do at a party with your ghoulfriends?

Scary Cute♥♥

JOHN PHILIP BOOSA

Dance your afternoon away to a rockin' march medley. Cue up some tunes by John Philip Boosa (known to the normies as John Philip Sousa) and break out the marching band dance moves. You may want to get some inspiration from pop goddess Gwen Spookani.

Draw your parade costume here!

Tips:

★ Choreograph in counts of eight.
★ Every ghoul should dance the same steps for real armed-forces flair.
★ Don't underestimate the power of salutes, marching in time, and high kicks.

SPOOKLER WRITING

When it's time for frighterworks, write your ghoulfriends' names in the night sky with spooklers. You'll definitely need adult supervision for this one. Try having contests to see who can write her name the fastest, who can write the longest sentence, who can write the largest, and who can write the smallest.

And with an adult's help, try taking pictures of your writing. You'll need a camera that you can set in night mode and that has the option for a long exposure. Even if the writing isn't clear, the pictures will be riveting!

I GOT MAD SKILLS

ROBECCA

Print out and paste
your favorite spookler
pictures here.

SCARISIAN FLING PARTY

According to paragraph 7.14 of the Gargoyle Code of Ethics, it is a gargoyle's responsibility to throw a claw-some Scarisian Fling at least once a year.

Lay out a *très chic* spread of croissants, chocolats, and sparkling grape juice, and add the red, white, and blue of the French flag. *Vive la France!*

Ghoul LA LA!

VOCABUSCARY

You need to learn un petit peu de français to skelebrate properly. Use the pronunciation guide below to sound out the phrases, then practice saying them with your ghoulfriends.

Yes	Oui (WHEE)
No	Non (NON)
Maybe	Peut-être (puh-TEH-truh)
Where are the bathrooms?	Où sont les toilettes? (OOH sawnt LAY twah-LET)
How much does that cost?	Combien ça coûte? (COM-bee-in sah COOT)
That's adorable!	C'est adorable! (say TA-doh-RAH-bluh)
What a surprise!	Quelle surprise! (KELL sir-PREEZE)
A little bit	Un petit peu (unh PUH-tee PUH)

What frightfully fabulous new adventures would you and your ghoulfriends have on a dream trip to Scaris? What sites would you see, and what would you eat?

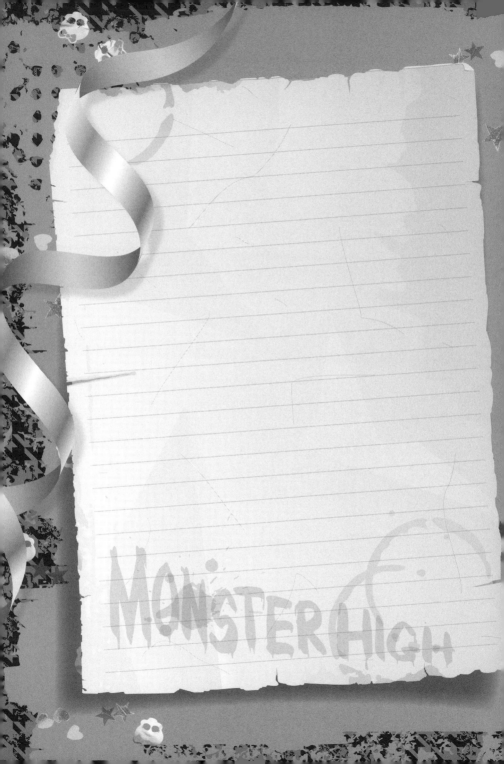

SO THIS CENTURY...

I GOT MAD SKILLS

HOWLOWEEN PARTY

Get your digs ghoulammed up for a spooktacular Howloween! Old-ghoul Howloween decorations? So bland! Make everything old new again by using craft supplies you have on hand to make your own ghoulamorous Howloween decorations with some well-placed accessories.

First, list some standard decorations:

★ pumpkins

★ ghosts

★ bats

★ witches

★ spiderwebs

★ _____

★ _____

★ _____

★ _____

★ _____

Then, list some fangtastic accessories and details:

- ★ hair bows
- ★ purses
- ★ zippers
- ★ safety pins
- ★ purple eyes

- ★ pink lips
- ★ lashes
- ★ _____
- ★ _____
- ★ _____

Next, gather your craft supplies:

- ★ construction paper in pink, black, white, orange, or other wild colors
- ★ glue
- ★ markers
- ★ scissors

- ★ wild ribbons (for hair bows)
- ★ _____
- ★ _____
- ★ _____
- ★ _____

Instructions:

1. Pick an item from the decorations list, like the pumpkin. Draw the pumpkin and cut it out.
2. Pick some items from the accessories and details list, like purple eyes and a purse. Draw these, cut them out, then glue them to the pumpkin.
3. Repeat steps one and two with different combinations!

You can do this before the party, or you can wait until your ghoulfriends arrive and create the decorations together!

HOWLOWEEN CHIC

CLAW
esome!

Before your ghoulfriends arrive, you need to get dolled up in a fangtastic Howloween costume. Will you be scary, or will you be scary-cute? You have a lot of options!

Costume Ideas:

★ fave monster ghoul
★ Casketball player
★ fave monster pet
★ fearleader
★ iCoffin

PARTY
TIL
THE full
MOON COMES
UP.

PASS THE PUMPKIN

Get your body moving like you're in a *Dead Fast* comic with a fangtastic relay race, Howloween-style. You'll need two pumpkins and some superhero reflexes.

Scary Cute

★ Divide into two even teams and line up facing forward (so each ghoul is looking at the fur of the ghoul in front of her). Ghoul A (the first ghoul in line) on each team starts out with her team's pumpkin.

★ Ghoul A passes the pumpkin over her head to Ghoul B. Ghoul B passes the pumpkin under her legs to Ghoul C.

★ Repeat this over/under pattern until the pumpkin reaches the last ghoul in line.

★ The last ghoul runs to the front of the line with the pumpkin and passes it back in the same way, until each ghoul has been at the front of the line.

★ Whichever team gets the original Ghoul A back to the front of the line first wins!

That was exhausting!

What's the spookiest party you've ever been to?

OTHER FREAKY FAB EVENTS

Did you get a new pet? Is it time for a fashion show? Did you get a surprise snow day? All of these freaky fab occasions call for a spooktacular party! Any reason for a party is a good reason for a party.

★ Roll out the red carpet for your gohulamorous self and your gohulamorous ghoulfriends.

★ The polterazzi (aka your scarents) will snap pics as everyone arrives in their est ensembles, and then it's party time.

★ You'll want red and gold decorations, plus ghoulamorous photos of your favorite stars adorning the walls.

★ Serve elegant finger foods, and ask your ghoulfriends to arrive in their red-carpet finest.

The Freakademy Awards have been given since 1929, so there's a long history of ghoulamorousness to live up to.

STARGAZING

When you're getting ghoulammed up for the party, you may want to use some of your favorite skelebrities as inspiration. Who are some creepy cool actors you admire?

Skelena Gomez
Zac Efright
Anne Hauntaway

Robert Phantomson
Ghoulia Roberts
Jenniscare Lawrence

CHIC CHARADES

Before the Freakademy votes, you'll want to show off your fangtastic acting skills. Play a few rounds of charades to prove you've got what it takes!

Instructions:

1. Divide into two teams. Each team writes titles of books, skelevision shows, movies, names of famous people, or common phrases or quotes on slips of paper and then folds them up. Each team then places their slips in a separate bowl.

2. The teams take turns, with one ghoul playing the actor at a time. The actor picks a slip of paper from the other team's bowl. Don't tell anyone what it says! Without speaking, the actor helps her team guess her word(s) by giving signals using appropriate gestures (see opposite page!). She has three minutes. (Set a timer on your iCoffin.)

3. The turn is over when the team guesses the title or time runs out, whichever happens first. No guesses from the other team!

4. The team with the most correct answers wins.

★ **Book title:** Put your hands together, then open them like a book.

★ **Film title:** Make an O with one hand to indicate a lens while cranking the other hand as if you are operating an old-fashioned movie camera.

★ **Skelevision show:** Make a box with your fingers.

★ **Quotes and phrases:** Make air quotes.

★ **Famous person:** Pose with your hands on your hips.

Word hints:

★ Pull on your ear to indicate that the word being guessed sounds like the word you are about to demonstrate.

★ Pinch or open your thumb and forefinger for a short or long word.

★ Use fingers to show the number of words in the answer; then use fingers to show which word you want your teammates to guess.

★ Hold fingers against your arm to show how many syllables are in a particular word.

★ Show that a word guessed is correct by tapping your index finger on your nose.

★ Wipe your hand across your forehead when the ghouls on your team are getting hot; cross your arms and shiver when they're getting cold.

FREAKADEMY AWARDS CEREMONY

Obviously, the highlight of the Freakademy Awards—right after the fashion, the ghoulossip, and more of the fashion—is finding out who wins each award! Pick a host to amp you up—this can be a ghoul, a guest, a scarent, or an obedient sibling. Let the ceremony commence!

First, you need to create some awards. Make a list of award ideas!

★ Beast Spooktress
★ Beast Deadrector
★ Beast Costume Design
★ _____
★ _____
★ _____
★ _____

Then, you need to make frightfully fancy award certificates. You can create these on your computer.

When you're ready for the ceremony, have your ghoulfriends write their names on identical slips of paper, fold them in half, and drop them in a hat. (Preferably a top hat—but any hat will do.)

The host will open the ceremony with a speech. Watch some award intros on FrightTube for inspiration, and write a speech for your host here.

After the introduction, it's time to hand out the awards. Read the award, then draw a name from the hat to find out who the winner is!

FREAKADEMY AWARD—WINNING

MOVIES

Finish off with a Freakademy Award viewing party. Make a list of movies that you consider award-worthy. To figure out what movie you'll watch, just put it to the vote!

Nominated Movies:

MONSTER PET PARTY

Pets are monsters too! Skelebrate them in style, decorating with paw prints, pet pics, and pet toys. And you can serve snacks in (new, unused) pet food dishes!

GHOULFRIEND TREATS

Make some easy snacks before the party so your ghoulfriends don't miss their feeding time. Try making this fur-and-feathers treat!

PUPPY CHOW

Puppy chow will fill you with puppy love! You'll need to refrigerate this for at least a few hours, so leave plenty of time to make it before your party.

You'll need:

* 1 cup peanut butter
* 12 ounces chocolate chips
* 1 stick margarine
* 1 box Crispix cereal
* 2½ cups powdered sugar
* clean paper grocery bag
* wax paper

Instructions:

1. Put the peanut butter, chocolate chips, and margarine in a bowl and microwave for 2 minutes. Then stir until melted.
2. Pour over the Crispix in a bowl. Mix well.
3. Put the sugar in a paper bag, add the Crispix mixture, and shake vigorously.
4. Spread on a cookie sheet covered with wax paper to cool.
5. Refrigerate to harden.

PARTY WITH YOUR PETS!

Where did you meet your pet?

What is your favorite memory with your pet?

What do you like beast about your pet?

If your pet could talk, what would she say to you?

Before the party, plug yourself into the
Internet and cue up the scary-cutest pet
videos you can find. Try searches for
some of these animals:

★ sloth   ★ kitten   ★ red panda
★ loris   ★ baby goat
★ sugar glider   ★ puppy

Jot down the names of your favorite videos here:

★ _____   ★ _____
★ _____   ★ _____
★ _____   ★ _____

Now search for these duos:
★ horse and cat
★ bear and dog
★ hamster and cat

Jot down the names of your favorite videos here:
_____ _____ _____ _____

GHOST PET

If you've always wanted a pet but can't have one, or if you have one and want it to have a friend, this is your chance. It's time for you to adopt a ghost pet! What kinds of pets would you like to have?

★ dragon   ★ gargoyle   ★ ferret

★ snake   ★ owl   ★ _____

★ _____   ★ _____   ★ _____

★ _____   ★ _____   ★ _____

★ _____   ★ _____   ★ _____

★ _____   ★ _____   ★ _____

FANGTASTIC PET BOOK

Fill out this fangtastic petbook for easy access to your Watzits' and Crescents' personal info.

To show off your pet's boo-nique nature, you'll need:

- ★ pictures of your pet
- ★ paw- and claw-shaped stencils
- ★ animal stickers
- ★ thought-bubble stencils or stickers

- ★ crayons and pencils
- ★ glue
- ★ scissors

PHOTOGENIC FAUNA

Paste photos of your pet's scary-cute mugs here! Add thought bubbles to capture their secret musings, and use the stencils, stickers, and crayons to embellish.

How old was your fuzzy friend when you met her?

How much does she weigh?

How would you describe what she looks like?

What cute things did she do as a baby?

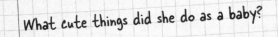

What is her favorite game?

What does her bark, meow, squawk, or roar sound like?

Who are her favorite monsters and normies? Why?

What else is important to you about your pet?

FREAKY CHIC FASHION SHOW PARTY

Show off your couture with a fashionable extravaganza. Drape your tables with folds of freaky chic fabric, plus vases filled with ribbons, lace, and feathers. Top it off with some fashion mags scattered about artfully.

Some fashions, like little black dresses and pearls, are classic. Others are wild flashes in the pan. Opaque tights...as pants? Old-timey monsterstaches...in the twenty-first century? Wearing a dress...made of meat? None of these trends will last. What are some of the funniest fashion faux-claws you can think of?

INSPIRATION

Get inspired by fashion magazines and websites. Look at fashion pictures, but also look at food, nature, sports—even ads. Each ghoul should write or draw her favorite ideas, then show them off to the group. Vote on the most creative, the weirdest, and the ghouliest. Use this page to fill in some of your own inspirations.

ARTIST, MONSTER, CLAY

Work together to make a monster sculpture with this claw-some game. You don't need any supplies for it!

Instructions:

1. Break into groups of three. (If anyone is left out, some ghouls can go twice.)

2. One group of three stands up; everyone else stays seated as the spooktators. One ghoul is the artist, one is the monster, and one is the piece of clay.

3. The clay faces the spooktators. It's very important that she never sees the monster.

4. The monster stands behind the artist and picks a pose. (Sitting, standing, kneeling, legs and arms straight, bent, crossed—be creative, but pick a pose you can hold for two or three minutes.)

5. The artist sculpts the clay into the same pose the monster is in. The artist cannot speak, mimic the monster's pose, or touch the clay. She should treat the clay as though the clay is an actual lump of clay or a block of marble, pushing and pulling and shaping the clay into the right shape. (But don't touch the clay!) See how close you can get to matching the monster's pose!

6. Set a timer for three minutes. When the time is up, take a picture of the clay and the monster so you can compare them!

FREAKY CHIC FASHION SHOW

To prep for your fashion show, pull some outfits from your closet. You can take fashion in a gazillion directions. Try some of these ideas and sketch more here.

★ monochromatic (one color head to claw)
★ each piece a different color
★ clashing patterns
★ baggy bottoms with fitted tops
★ fitted bottoms with baggy tops
★ as many layers as you can manage

FREAKY CHIC FASHION SHOW

Have your ghoulfriends bring their most skelacious wardrobe pieces—tops, skirts, shoes, boas, jewels; add your own; and pool it all together. Then put together skella-cool, totally boo-nique, unexpected ensembles. Pick a killer soundtrack, strut down the runway, and then do it all over again!

Make a list of the songs you want to listen to.
* "Rolling in the Creep"
* "What Makes You Boo-tiful"
* "One More Fright"

FASHION SHOW TIPS

★ Lay some ribbon out on the floor to outline the runway.

★ Blast your claw-some soundtrack.

★ Be each other's spooktators: Break into two groups. One group will watch while the other group lines up to take turns strutting down the catwalk. Then switch.

★ Walk the runway one ghoul at a time. When you get to the end, strike a pose and wait for the applause to die down. Then execute a graceful turn and sashay back up the runway.

GHOUL DS. FRIENDS FOREVER

MAD SCIENCE IN THE FAB PARTY

Living in the Fab is totally voltage: mad fashion plus mad science! Deck your house out like a glittery science lab, complete with beakers and lab coats, and set out some minty green desserts. Albert Frightstein, Marie Cursie, and Nikola Terrorsla would be proud!

FREAKY FAB

THE GHOSTLY FLOAT EXPERIMENT

You'll need:

★ 1 egg
★ 1 packet each of ketchup, mustard, and soy sauce (from a restaurant)
★ water
★ kosher salt (kosher so the water will stay clear)
★ a tall drinking glass

Instructions:

1. Pour water into the glass until it is about half full.
2. Stir in about six tablespoons of salt.
3. Carefully pour in plain water until the glass is nearly full. Don't disturb or mix the salt water with the plain water.
4. Gently lower the egg into the water.

What just happened? Well, salt water is denser than freshwater, and objects float better in denser liquids. When you lower the egg into the liquid, it drops through the normal tap water until it reaches the salty water, at which point the water is dense enough for the egg to float.

Now try some experiments with this project. Fill the glass with straight salt water and try placing the egg in. Where does it float? What about the packets of ketchup, mustard, and soy sauce? Do they float at different heights? Does changing the water temperature have any effect?

Variable: _____
Result: _____
Notes: _____

_____
_____

Variable: _____
Result: _____
Notes: _____

_____
_____

Variable: _____
Result: _____
Notes: _____

_____
_____

Variable: _____
Result: _____
Notes: _____

_____
_____
_____

POLTER-PENNIES EXPERIMENT

Divide into groups of a few ghouls each and test your powers of deaduction with this polter-pennies experiment.

You'll need:

- ★ 10 old (not shiny) pennies
- ★ 10 old quarters
- ★ 10 old dimes
- ★ 10 old nickels
- ★ several nuts and bolts
- ★ 1/4 cup white vinegar
- ★ 1/4 cup orange juice
- ★ 1/4 cup lemon juice
- ★ 1 teaspoon salt
- ★ non-metal bowl
- ★ paper towels

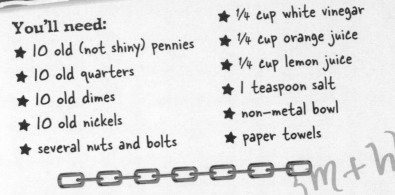

Polter-Penny Demonstration 1:

1. Pour the vinegar into the bowl, add the salt, and stir.
2. Put five pennies in the bowl, and slowly count to ten.
3. Take out the pennies, and rinse them in some water.
4. Shiny and clean!

What just happened? Vinegar contains acid, and the acid in the vinegar reacts with the salt to remove the copper oxide that was making your pennies so uggo.

Variable:

Result:

Notes:

Variable:

Result:

Notes:

Variable:

Result:

Notes:

Variable:

Result:

Notes:

Polter-Penny Demonstration 2:

1. Put five more pennies in the bowl, and slowly count to ten again.
2. Take them out, but *don't* rinse them. Place them on a paper towel to dry.
3. Wait long enough, and the pennies will turn bluish green, because malachite, a chemical, will form.

Polter-Penny Demonstration 3

1. Put the nuts and bolts in the vinegar you just used. They may turn copper, because the vinegar removed some of the copper from the pennies, and the copper will then be attracted to the metal in the nuts and bolts.

Polter-Penny: Further Experiments

Now you know what happens when you put dirty pennies in a salt-and-vinegar solution. But what would happen if you change some of the variables?

1. Try the above again with other acidic liquids, like lemon juice or orange juice.
2. Try it with nickels, dimes, and quarters.
3. Try changing the amount of salt you add to the solution.
4. Record your scientific observations on the next page.

Variable:

Result:

Notes:

Variable:

Result:

Notes:

Variable:

Result:

Notes:

Variable:

Result:

Notes:

FEARBOOK MEETING PARTY

When the school year starts wrapping up, you know what that means: It's time to call a Fearbook meeting, ghouls! Get the sports, gossip, clubs, and photography staff members together to create a Fearbook that will put all the Fearbooks in the history of Monster High to shame.

Fearbooks help you revisit all the things that happened over the past year. What are some of your favorite things about Fearbooks?

Look through your old Fearbooks. Maybe you even have them all the way back to kindergarten! What spooktacular memories do your old Fearbooks trigger?

What things are different now than they were in your old Fearbooks?

PHARAOH'S PHOTO BOOTH

Come to the party picture-ready and take some pharaohific on-the-spot Fearbook pics in the photo booth.

You'll need:

★ several different patterned cloths or papers for backgrounds (Brocade, polka dots, and stars are all great choices.)

★ camera

★ color printer and photo paper

Oh My Rah

You'll also need photo booth props. Try some of the props below, and add some of your own to the list.

Props:
- ★ tiara
- ★ wand
- ★ pom-poms
- ★ sports equipment
- ★ schoolbooks or binders
- ★ a large fake chicken
- ★ garden gnome
- ★ cauldron
- ★ beakers
- ★ feather boas

- ★ capes
- ★ fedoras
- ★ _____
- ★ _____
- ★ _____
- ★ _____
- ★ _____
- ★ _____
- ★ _____

Now jump into the photo booth solo or in groups, trick yourselves out with props, and snap away. Pick your favorite pics to print out for posterity.

The most important way to leave your mark on the Fearbook is by designing a ghoulamorous cover. Try out some furocious cover designs here!

GAME FRIGHT PARTY

Break out the cards and board games! Decorate in red and black, and scatter some red and black playing cards on the tables to match. Board games and card games are often beast for four players, so you will probably want to invite either three friends and all play together or seven friends and play in groups (mixing up the groups for each game).

Whether it's a game of skill or a game of chance— or a combination of both—card and board games are a scary-fun way to hexercise your brain. What are some of your favorite games to play?

SLAPJACK(SON)

Instructions:

1. Deal the entire deck of cards facedown. Don't look at your cards; they stay facedown throughout.
2. The ghoul to the dealer's left turns the card on top of her stack faceup in the center of the table.
3. Play continues with ghouls placing their cards faceup in the center of the table.
4. When a Jack(son) is played, all ghouls try to be the first to slap their hand on the stack.
5. The first ghoul to slap the stack gets to take it and add it to the bottom of her stack of cards.

6. The ghoul to the left of the slapper starts a new pile in the center.
7. The game ends when one ghoul gets all the cards.

Rules:

★ If a ghoul loses all her cards, she has one chance to get back in the game: The next time a Jack(son) is played, if she's the first to slap, she's back in. If she isn't, then she's officially out.

★ If multiple ghouls slap the Jack(son), the ghoul with her hand at the bottom gets the cards. No using fingernails, ghouls!

★ If a ghoul slaps a card that isn't a Jack(son), she has to give the ghoul who played that card one of her own cards.

PARLIAMONSTER

Deal the entire deck of cards. For this game, you do need to look at your cards: Sort them into sequences in each suit.

1. The ghoul with the seven of diamonds starts by placing this card in the middle. The game continues with each ghoul, if possible, adding a diamond card to the sequence. The sequence can either go up (eight, nine, ten, and so on) or down (six, five, four, and so on).

2. These cards are placed on either side of the seven, in order, so the diamonds form a row.

3. If you don't have the correct diamond card, you can start a new sequence in a different suit by placing any of the other sevens below the seven of diamonds, starting a new row for that suit. If you don't have the correct diamond or another seven, you skip your turn.

4. The winner is the first ghoul to use all her cards, although the remaining ghouls can continue until all four rows are complete.

Give yourself 5 points every time you win a round of Slapjack(son) or Parliamonster. Keep track of your scores to see who's the most skilled card spark!

GHOUL NAME					
ROUND ONE					
ROUND TWO					
ROUND THREE					
ROUND FOUR					
ROUND FIVE					
ROUND SIX					
ROUND SEVEN					
ROUND EIGHT					
ROUND NINE					
ROUND TEN					
TOTALS					

FREAKY FAB

GHOUL NAME					
ROUND ONE					
ROUND TWO					
ROUND THREE					
ROUND FOUR					
ROUND FIVE					
ROUND SIX					
ROUND SEVEN					
ROUND EIGHT					
ROUND NINE					
ROUND TEN					
TOTALS					

SCREAM TEAM

PARTY REVIEW: OTHER FREAKY FAB EVENTS

What special boo-casions did you skelebrate? What special boo-nique touches did you add to make the party your own? What would you do differently next time? Write all about it here!

GHOUL NERD

FOR YOUR GHOUL-FRIENDS

Ghoulfriends are forever! You always need to have your ghouls' backs, and that includes throwing parties for them to skelebrate the end of finals, to help them update their wardrobes, or just because you think a party would make their weekend. That's what ghoulfriends are for!

PRETTY SCARY T-SHIRT PARTY

If you've never used your creative fires to design your own clothes, now is the time to start. Ask your ghoulfriends to each bring a T-shirt to decorate. Cover your table with paper tablecloths (dab some artful paint blobs on them) and set out a stack of palettes and some jars of paintbrushes. Don't forget snacks—"starving artist" is a cliché you can live without!

You'll need:
★ T-shirts (plain white shirts or shirts with colors or patterns; whichever you want!)
★ fabric pencils
★ thread
★ sewing needles
★ scissors
★ measuring tape
★ embellishments of your choice

You'll use the measuring tape and fabric pencils to mark where you want to cut, paint, or add embellishments.

DRAGONTASTIC DESIGNS

With a T-shirt and your sewing and craft supplies, you'll have a freaky fabulous designer piece that is 100 percent you. But before you put your claws on any fabric, you need to figure out what you want to make. Using pencil and paper, draw some T-shirt design ideas.

Design Tips:

★ Remember that you can use scissors to cut Vs and scallops along the neck, cuffs, and bottom of your shirt.

★ Try a simple pattern, like a bright-colored straight line down the center of the shirt, or something more complex, like squiggles everyscare!

★ Add some embellishments! You can try buttons, ribbons, lace, fabric patches, embroidery, acrylic paint, braided fabric, and more.

Draw some of your design ideas here!

CLAWARD CEREMONY

After you finish your monsterpieces, show off your creations and vote for some claw-some awards. Give the awards below and include some award ideas of your own.

★ Most Boo-nique
★ Spookiest Style
★ Most Skelegant

★ Beast All-Around
★ Dragontella Versace Achievement Award

FANGERNATIONAL GHOULS OF MYSTERY PARTY

Sometimes a ghoul's got some spying to do, and she doesn't want anyone to know about it. A spooky spy party is a great place to learn how to snoop around. Decorate with some incognito black and white, add some spy silhouettes to the walls, and prep a table with spy supplies for your ghoulfriends: oversize sunglasses, magnifying glasses, and notepads with mini pens.

GHOULS IN DISGUISE

The first step to being a spy is learning to go undercover. Trench coats are old hat, of course, but a ghoul needs to have some other options up her fins, so I always like to make monsterstaches!

You'll need:

★ black, brown, red, and yellow felt
★ paper
★ scissors
★ pencils
★ permanent markers
★ glue
★ straws
★ sequins and glitter (optional)

Instructions:

1. Draw the monsterstache of your choice.
2. Cut out the monsterstache shape from your tracing paper.

3. Using the tracing paper as a stencil, draw the monsterstache shape onto your felt with a permanent marker.

4. Cut out your monsterstache.
5. If you want your disguise to have a sparkly spirit, glue sequins or glitter to your 'stache.

Now you have an instant spooky disguise!

6. Glue the straw to the back of your monsterstache as a handle. (On the right side if you're right-handed; on the left side if you're left-handed.)

CREEP A SECRET

All spies have to communicate in code, of course, to protect their secrets. And you can never learn too many codes! Check this one out.

Write your message backward:

!edoc retsnom terces ym si sihT

But that isn't disguised very well, so add a random letter and number before each character, like this:

!x7ek2dj7ot6cm9
rd1ew3tl8sh7nd4ob2md5
tv7ea4rf6cr3eb9sql yu6mg8 sp7ih4
sm9iz2hr6Tfl

The message is "This is my secret monster code!"

Now write some secret messages to your ghoulfriends!

GHOUL NERD

Now that you have secret messages to give one another, you have to figure out how to transfer them without getting caught. Eat some snacks, gossip, and try out one another's monsterstaches—and try to pass your message to your asset without anyone else noticing. (You'll want to fold it up very small, so it's hard for anyone to see.) Can you pass your message without anyone finding out?

My BESTIE

Here are some monster methods to try:

★ Make eye contact with your asset when no one else is looking so that she knows you're trying to get the message to her.

★ Hand your contact a snack, a hair band, or an iCoffin—along with the message, hidden in your palm.

★ Put the message in between the pages of a magazine, book, or newspaper, and set it down somewhere.
Make sure your asset sees you doing it, but act casual.

★ When your asset is looking at you, drop something (along with the message), and let her pick it up for you. Try to make it seem like an accident.

What are some other tricks you can try?

After everyone has passed her message (or been caught trying), it's time to decode them and read them out loud!

GUESS THE GHOUL

Identifying clues is a key part of both spying and journalism. Can you recognize clues your ghoulfriends leave behind?

You'll need:
★ white paper
★ pink marker
★ pencil

Instructions:

1. With the marker, trace your left hand (even if you're left-handed) on a sheet of paper. Everyone needs to share the same marker so the color will be identical!

2. Write your name lightly in pencil on the back of your sheet.

3. Gather all the sheets together and mix them up. Spread the sheets out on a table or the floor or hang them on the wall. Number the sheets.

4. Now, on another sheet of paper, write down who you think each hand belongs to.

5. Once everyone has guessed, turn the hand outlines over to see which hand goes with which ghoul!

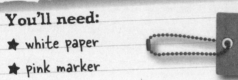

SKE-LASER COURSE

Anything worth sneaking out of a museum to thwart a villain's nefarious plan to steal it is going to be well guarded, possibly even with ske-lasers. Can you make it through the ske-laser field without touching any lasers?

In a hallway, tape hot-pink crepe paper or yarn in a laser pattern; like the one below.

Each ghoul has three minutes to get through the ske-laser field without touching any ske-lasers.

GHOULADUATION SKELEBRATION

Once the ghoul year is over, you will be a ghouladuate! Skelebrate your achievement with a big old party—Monster High–style! Decorate everything you can get your hands on with your school colors, set out a celebratory feast, and go cuh-razy!

Ghouladuation is a sign of moving onward and upward. What are some goals you hope to achieve by the time ghouladuation from your current school year rolls around?

_____

_____

_____

_____

_____

_____

TIME CAPSULE

I wish I really could capture time!
But at least you can capture time
that's in the past. Make a capsule for any mementos
you want to keep from the past school year.

You'll need:

★ a shoebox
★ scissors
★ tape
★ colorful magazines
★ glue
★ markers

Instructions:

1. Fill your shoebox with mementos and other paranormalia you'll want to take a peek at in the future.
2. Wrap the shoebox and lid separately, using pages from the magazines. Make the capsule as neat and beautiful as you can.
3. Draw ghoulgeous designs all over the box.

What capital paranormalia will you put in your time capsule?

Draw some time-capsule box designs here!

What party did you throw for your ghoulfriends? And what would be the ultimate dream party to throw for (or with!) them?

MONSTER HIGH